W9-AHJ-572

MISSIONS OF THE U.S.
MARINE FORCE RECON

BY BRANDON TERRELL

Published by The Child's World®
1980 Lookout Drive • Mankato, MN 56003-1705
800-599-READ • www.childsworld.com

Acknowledgments
The Child's World®: Mary Berendes, Publishing Director
Red Line Editorial: Design, editorial direction, and production
Photographs ©: Sgt. Christopher Q. Stone/U.S. Marine Corps, cover, 1; Lance Cpl. Tyler Dietrich/U.S. Marine Corps, 5; Sgt. Jacob N. Bailey/U.S. Air Force, 6; Lance Cpl. Brennan O'Lowney/U.S. Marine Corps, 8; MSgt. J. W. Richardson/U.S. Marine Corps History Division, 10; HO/DOD/AP Images, 12; Lance Cpl. James J. Vooris/U.S. Marine Corps, 14; Lance Cpl. Kenneth E. Madden III/U.S. Marine Corps, 16; Sgt. Ezekiel Kitandwe/U.S. Marine Corps, 18; Cpl. Chad J. Pulliam/U.S. Marine Corps, 20; Sgt. Kimberly Hackbarth/U.S. Department of Defense, 21

ISBN 9781634074452

LCCN 2015946359

Printed in the United States of America
Mankato, MN
December, 2015
PA02285

TABLE OF CONTENTS

ABOUT THE U.S. MARINE FORCE RECON

- The United States Marine Force Reconnaissance (also called Force Recon or FORECON) was founded in 1957.
- More than 2,000 active Recon Marines currently serve in the U.S. Marine Corps.
- The primary role of a Force Recon Marine is to gather intelligence in support of the Marine Corps. This is done by conducting:
  - » **amphibious** reconnaissance: surveying areas around water and oceans;
  - » battle space shaping: moving the enemy to where you would like them to be;
  - » ground reconnaissance: surveying areas on land; and
  - » surveillance: keeping a watchful eye for enemies.

- There are two types of Force Recon missions:
    - » Black Operations: conducting direct-action missions, such as getting on an enemy ship;
    - » Green Operations: collecting intelligence, observing, and reporting without being seen.
- Force Recon's motto: "Swift, Silent, Deadly."

CHAPTER 1

CAMP PENDLETON, CALIFORNIA

"Atten-tion!"

The commanding officer, or CO, looked at the group of new marines. The marines stood in rows.

"Welcome to Basic Recon Course," said the CO.

Basic Recon Course is 12 extremely hard weeks of

◄ **Marines stand at attention in straight rows, arms at their sides and feet together.**

training. In the end, the **recruits** would be Force Recon soldiers. "Are you up to the challenge?!"

"Sir, yes, sir!" the marines shouted.

In his gruff voice, the CO told them about their training. He told them it would focus on strength and endurance. They would have many tests. Run obstacle courses. Tread water in full combat gear. Parachute and hang by rope from helicopters. All of these tests would push them to their limits.

The CO explained that these marines would face the longest days of their lives. He described an 18-hour endurance test. Part of the test included a swim. Each man would have an 80-pound (36-kg) bag strapped on. They would work in teams to run and row. They would also swim together while carrying a raft on their shoulders.

The CO looked around. No one moved. Not even when he told them how they would train at night in full combat simulations. They would have to learn to use full scuba gear. They would perfect their aiming, hiding, and communications skills. They would need to keep their minds focused and strong.

The CO paused. He moved back to his place in front of them all. "Now, let's get to work!" he growled.

CHAPTER 2

HAPPY VALLEY, VIETNAM

The jungle was full of surprises. First Force Recon Company trudged on. It was July 1967. They were going through Suoi Ca Valley in Vietnam. The area was also known as Happy Valley. But no one found anything happy about it.

The Force Recon team had flown into the valley. They climbed down ropes from

◀ Marines scout the jungle.

their helicopter to the jungle floor. It was now their second day of recon patrol. They were running a screening **operation**. This meant it was their job to scout. They were in charge of making sure it was safe for the other marines to enter the area.

They walked single file through tall weeds. Suddenly, their point man threw a hand into the air. The team was immediately silent. They crouched in the weeds. Through the trees came the sound of voices.

The point man dug out his map. He determined that there were no "friendlies" nearby. The voices had to be the enemy. They were surely North Vietnamese soldiers. And this meant they were making a run for weapons.

The team split. Four men rushed forward to stop the enemy. The rest hung back. The four took their positions. They spied the enemy carrying wooden crates.

The team aimed their weapons through the weeds. They set their sights just above the Vietnamese soldiers' heads.

In an instant, the jungle boomed with gunfire. *Rat-a-tat-a-tat!*

The enemy dropped their supplies. They scrambled for cover. It was clear they could not tell where the gunfire was coming from.

▲ One marine checks the map while another keeps his weapon at the ready.

One of the marines pulled the pin from a grenade. He threw it near the enemy.

KA-BOOM!

A section of the jungle blew up in shreds.

The marines fired for another minute or two. Finally they stopped.

Silence.

The path was empty.

The enemy had **retreated**.

The Force Recon team met next to the smoking crater the grenade had left. Broken crates were scattered around them. Weapons and supplies littered the road.

The point man crouched down. He pried open a cracked crate. Inside was a long, detailed list of enemy codes. They searched other crates and found food, medical supplies, gas masks, and weapons.

It was the largest stock of supplies and weapons any of them had ever seen.

The jungle was full of surprises. And not all of its surprises were bad.

CHAPTER 3

GRENADA, CARIBBEAN SEA

The enemy had taken control of the governor's mansion in Saint George's. The enemy was the People's Revolution Army. A team of Navy SEALs was pinned down there. Their gear was left on their helicopter. Their only radio was out of battery power. They had called in for support using a phone from inside the mansion. The year was 1983.

◀ **Marines rush toward the governor's mansion during the Grenada Invasion of 1983.**

Five tanks, 13 amphibious vehicles, and 250 marines were sent to help. They were coming from the USS *Guam*. This was a U.S. ship in the Atlantic Ocean. The **platoon** made its way to the governor's mansion. Day was breaking over the island.

The house was red and white. It sat perched on a hill. It had two stories. Inside, along with the Navy SEALs, were a number of government officials. The Force Recon Marines moved toward the house. Gunfire broke out.

The People's Revolution Army had turned their weapons on the marines. The marines fired back and closed in on the house. They pushed the enemy back. Then they made their way inside the building.

The Navy SEALs were happy to see the marines. They gathered the government officials and got ready to leave. Some enemy soldiers gave up their weapons. Others fled into the jungles outside the city. A helicopter arrived to bring the officials out. Together with the Navy SEALs, the Marine Force Recon team had successfully finished its mission.

CHAPTER 4

FALLUJAH, IRAQ

It was after nightfall. Fallujah, Iraq, was quiet on this 2004 night. Suddenly, explosions shook the streets. Flashes of white light lit up mud, stone, and brick buildings. Laundry hanging on lines flapped in the wind. Smoke rose into the starry sky.

Twenty-four Marine Force Recon team members had come into the city. Their team leader had just called in the **airstrike**. They hid in foxholes dug into the

◀ **Marine Force Recon members in Fallujah huddle behind a wall and wait for further instructions.**

hard-packed earth. From the holes, they watched the explosions rain down on the city.

In two days, nearly 12,000 U.S. and Iraqi forces would invade Fallujah. Rebels were running the city. They had weapons stashed throughout. And they hid in the shadows. They were everywhere and nowhere at once. They needed to be stopped.

A missile flashed overhead. Another building exploded. Chunks of mud, stone, and brick crumbled in the street.

As the dust cleared, the Force Recon team members leapt from their foxholes. Their weapons were ready. They moved together into the street.

The front doors of an apartment building opened before them. The team leader directed his troops inside. The marines made their way up the steps one at a time. Finally they all reached the fourth floor. The apartment door stood open. The team quickly swarmed inside. They checked the apartment. It was empty.

They unstrapped their helmets and gave themselves a moment to relax. The team's **sniper** lay on his belly. He propped his weapon up on a tripod. It was aimed outside the open window. Now they would wait.

It was the job of the Force Recon platoon to shape the battle space before it began. They had to stop the enemy from getting supplies. It was their job to move the enemies like chess pieces. The marines would move the enemy right where they wanted them. And that is just what the airstrike did. It moved the enemy out of the area. Now the Force Recon team could work on taking control of the city.

The city of Fallujah was quiet once more. But it wouldn't be for long.

◀ **A Marine Force Recon soldier takes his position.**

CHAPTER 5

MOUNTAIN ROAD, AFGHANISTAN

Through night-vision goggles, the dangerous mountains ahead glowed green like monsters. The packs the marines wore on their backs weighed at least 100 pounds (45 kg) each. They were filled with supplies, food, water, batteries, and

◀ **In enemy territory, marines travel at night using night-vision goggles to see.**

communication equipment. No one complained. It was all part of the job. They were trained for this.

The trek was brutal. Razor-sharp rocks and steep mountains were worse than any obstacle course. At the base of the mountain was a gravel road. It was the only path through this section of the mountains. The Force Recon platoon's job was to keep it safe.

In two days, a group of vehicles would be traveling on the road. Enemies had been spotted placing improvised explosive devices (IEDs) on the roads. If one of the trucks ran over an IED, it would set off a large bomb.

As the sun began to rise over the jagged mountains, the marines stopped hiking. They were 50 miles (80 km) from base and anyone friendly. They hunkered down in some rocks. Each marine slipped on a ghillie suit. The netted suits looked like grass and leaves. The marines now blended into the landscape.

They gathered leaves and added them to their suits. Then they hid in the bushes. They aimed their weapons at the road. Now they waited, watching and resting.

By afternoon, the sun scorched the desert sand around them. By now the Force Recon unit had moved three times. It was then

▲ Ghillie suits help camouflage soldiers.

that one of the marines spied something along the road. It was an IED.

He relayed the information to the platoon's communicator. It was the communicator's job to tell other marines their positions. It was also his job to say exactly where the bomb was hidden.

Soon, the sun dipped behind the mountains again. The heat of the day was over. This was a small relief after a long day. But there was no time to rest. Their job was not done. There were miles of roads left to watch and protect. Force Recon members went back to work as night blanketed the quiet desert.

▲ A soldier uses a metal detector to find a potential IED in Afghanistan.

GLOSSARY

airstrike (AIRSTRIKE): An airstrike is an attack or bombing made from the air. The Force Recon team leader in Fallujah, Iraq, called in an airstrike to support his ground troops.

amphibious (am-FIB-ee-uhs): Amphibious operations are carried out by land and sea forces acting together. During amphibious recon, members survey areas around land and water.

operation (ah-puh-RAY-shuhn): An operation is a military action or mission that includes planning. In Happy Valley, Vietnam, team members ran a screening operation.

platoon (pluh-TOON): A platoon is a group of soldiers made up of two or more squads. The platoon stormed the government house in Grenada in 1983.

recruits (ri-KROOTS): Recruits are people who have recently joined the armed forces. After training, the recruits would become marines.

retreated (ri-TREET-ud): Retreated means to have moved back or withdrawn from a difficult situation. The enemies in Happy Valley, Vietnam, retreated after the marines fired.

sniper (SNIPE-er): A sniper is a person who shoots from a hidden place. The sniper set up in an abandoned apartment in Fallujah, Iraq.

TO LEARN MORE

Books

Bozzo, Linda. *U.S. Special Forces*. Mankato, MN: Amicus Publishing, 2014.

Sandler, Michael. *Marine Force Recon in Action*. New York: Bearport Publishing, 2008.

Whiting, Jim. *Marine Corps Forces Special Operations Command*. Mankato, MN: Creative Education, 2015.

Web Sites

Visit our Web site for links about missions of the U.S. Marine Force Recon: childsworld.com/links

Note to Parents, Teachers, and Librarians: We routinely verify our Web links to make sure they are safe and active sites. So encourage your readers to check them out!

SELECTED BIBLIOGRAPHY

"Force RECON Training. "*Military.com*. Military.com, 2015. Web. 3 June 2015.

Hearn, Chester G. *Marines: An Illustrated History*. St. Paul, MN: Zenith Press, 2007.

Markowitz, Mark. "Urgent Fury: U.S. Special Operations Forces in Grenada, 1983." *Defense Media Network*. Defense Media Network, 3 June 2013. Web. 5 June 2015.

Ricks, Thomas E. *Making the Corps*. New York: Scribner, 2007.

INDEX

ABOUT THE AUTHOR

Brandon Terrell is the author of numerous children's books, with topics ranging from sports to spooky stories to swashbuckling adventures. When not hunched over his laptop writing, Terrell enjoys watching movies, reading, and spending time with his wife and two children.